Monstruos extintos/Extinct Monsters

El tigre de Tasmania

Tasmanian Tiger

por/by Janet Riehecky

Traducción/Translation: Dr. Martín Luís Guzmán Ferrer

Consultor en lectura/Reading Consultant: Barbara J. Fox
Reading Specialist
North Carolina State University

Consultor en contenidos/Content Consultant: Dr. Richard Gillespie
Visiting Fellow, Department of Archaeology and Natural History
Australian National University, Canberra

Capstone
press

Mankato, Minnesota

Blazers is published by Capstone Press,
151 Good Counsel Drive, P.O. Box 669, Mankato, Minnesota 56002.
www.capstonepress.com

Library of Congress Cataloging-in-Publication Data
Riehecky, Janet, 1953–
    [Tasmanian tiger Spanish & English]
    El tigre de Tasmania / por Janet Riehecky = Tasmanian tiger / by
Janet Riehecky.
    p. cm. — (Monstruos extintos = extinct monsters)
    Includes index.
    ISBN-13: 978-1-4296-0617-2 (hardcover)
    ISBN-10: 1-4296-0617-7 (hardcover)
    1. Thylacine — Juvenile literature. I. Title. II. Title: Tasmanian tiger.
III. Series.
QL737.M336R5418 2008
599.2'7 — dc22   2007031430

Summary: Simple text and illustrations describe Tasmanian tigers, how they
    lived, and how they became extinct — in both English and Spanish.

Editorial Credits
Jenny Marks, editor; Ted Williams, set designer; Jon Hughes and Russell
    Gooday/www.pixelshack.com, illustrators; Wanda Winch, photo researcher;
    Katy Kudela, bilingual editor; Eida del Risco, Spanish copy editor;
    Danielle Ceminsky, book designer

Photo Credits
Nature Picture Library/Dave Watts, 29 (Tasmanian tiger)
Shutterstock/Evan Enbom, 26–27 (paddock and background); Geoffrey Jewett,
    cover (nighttime background); N Joy Neish, 26 (windmill); Ronald
    Sumners, 24–25 (Australian outback)

1 2 3 4 5 6 13 12 11 10 09 08

For Josh, with love from Aunt Janet.

Table of Contents

Tabla de contenidos

Ancient Australia/ Hace mucho tiempo en Australia

About 30 million years ago, a weird, fierce beast prowled the wild lands of Australia.

Hace cerca de 30 millones de años, una bestia extraña y feroz merodeaba por las tierras salvajes de Australia.

The strange beast had
a strong, lean body. It looked
like a mix of tiger, wolf,
and kangaroo.

Esa extraña bestia tenía
un cuerpo fuerte y delgado.
Parecía una mezcla de tigre,
lobo y canguro.

The Tasmanian tiger was a top predator. This mysterious creature was one of the very largest meat-eating marsupials.

Monster Fact

Scientists named the Tasmanian tiger "Thylacine cynocephalus." The name means "pouched dog with a wolf's head."

Datos sobre el monstruo

Los científicos le pusieron al tigre de Tasmania "Thylacinus cynocephalus". El nombre quiere decir "perro con bolsa y cabeza de lobo".

El tigre de Tasmania era un excelente cazador. Esta misteriosa criatura era uno de los marsupiales carnívoros más grandes.

Weird and Wild/ Extraño y salvaje

The Tasmanian tiger had a wolflike body and soft, light brown fur. Dark brown stripes stretched across its back. Its long, stiff tail did not wag.

10

El tigre de Tasmania tenía un cuerpo parecido al de un lobo y una piel suave de color marrón claro. En su lomo se extendían largas rayas marrones. Su cola, alargada y tiesa, no se meneaba.

Tasmanian tigers were 2 feet (.6 meters) tall and 4 feet (1.2 meters) long. They weighed about 65 pounds (30 kilograms).

Los tigres de Tasmania medían 0.6 metros (2 pies) de alto y 1.2 metros (4 pies) de largo. Pesaban cerca de 30 kilos (65 libras).

Monster Fact

The Tasmanian tiger's bark sounded like a short, husky cough.

Datos sobre el monstruo

El ladrido del tigre de Tasmania sonaba como una tos ronca y breve.

The Tasmanian tiger had a strong jaw that opened an amazing 120 degrees. When their mouths snapped shut, their 46 sharp teeth cut like scissors.

El tigre de Tasmania tenía unas fuertes mandíbulas que asombrosamente se abrían 120 grados. Cuando su boca mordía y se cerraba rápidamente, sus 46 dientes filosos cortaban como tijeras.

Tasmanian tigers usually gave
birth to litters of three pups.
The blind, hairless pups stayed
in their mother's belly pouch until
they were a few months old.

Los tigres de Tasmania
generalmente tenían camadas
de tres cachorros. Los cachorros,
ciegos y sin pelo, se quedan en
la bolsa de la madre hasta que
tenían varios meses de nacidos.

Top Tiger/
El rey de los tigres

Tigers were unstoppable nighttime hunters. Many believe tigers chased their prey until the exhausted animal fell. The tiger's deadly bite finished the job.

Los tigres eran unos cazadores nocturnos imposibles de detener. Muchos piensan que estos tigres perseguían a su presa hasta que el exhausto animal caía. La mordida mortal del tigre hacía el resto.

Tasmanian tigers dined on small animals like birds, wombats, and wallabies. Some scientists think groups of tigers tackled larger animals like kangaroos.

El tigre de Tasmania comía animales pequeños como pájaros, wombats y ualabís. Algunos científicos creen que los tigres atacaban en grandes grupos a los animales de mayor tamaño, como los canguros.

Tasmanian tigers weren't always on the prowl. They took shelter in caves, hollow logs, and thick bushes.

Los tigres de Tasmania no siempre estaban al acecho. Se refugiaban en cuevas, troncos huecos y plantas muy frondosas.

A Monster Disappears/ El monstruo desaparece

For years, Tasmanian tigers thrived in Australia. Ancient people drew pictures of these beasts on cave walls. Then, 3,000 years ago, the tigers began to disappear.

Durante muchos años, los tigres prosperaron en Australia. La gente de la antigüedad dibujó a estas bestias en las paredes de las cavernas. Luego, hace como 3,000 años, los tigres empezaron a desaparecer.

By the 1930s, tigers were only found in Tasmania, an Australian island. Ranchers there claimed tigers killed their sheep. People hunted Tasmanian tigers until none were left.

En 1930, sólo era posible encontrar a estos tigres en Tasmania, una isla australiana. Los ganaderos decían que los tigres mataban a sus ovejas. Las personas los cazaron hasta que desaparecieron.

27

The last known Tasmanian tiger lived in the Beaumaris Zoo in Hobart, Tasmania. This animal died September 7, 1936. The tiger was named Benjamin.

El último tigre de Tasmania del que se tiene noticia vivía en el Zoológico Beaumaris de Hobart, Tasmania. Este animal murió el 7 de septiembre de 1936. El tigre se llamaba Benjamín.

Monster Fact

Scientists were unable to recreate a Tasmanian tiger by cloning one.

Datos sobre el monstruo

Los científicos no pudieron recrear un tigre de Tasmania por medio de la clonación.

Benjamin/ Benjamín

clone — to use an animal's cells to create another identical animal

litter — a group of animals born at the same time to one mother

marsupial—an animal that carries its young in a pouch

pouch — a flap of skin that looks like a pocket in which some animals carry their young

predator — an animal that lives by hunting other animals for food

prey — an animal that is hunted by another animal for food

prowl — to move around quietly and secretly

thrive — to live easily and well

wallaby — an Australian animal that looks like a small kangaroo

weird — strange or mysterious

wombat — an Australian animal that looks like a small bear

Internet Sites

FactHound offers a safe, fun way to find Internet sites related to this book. All of the sites on FactHound have been researched by our staff.

Here's how:
1. Visit *www.facthound.com*
2. Choose your grade level.
3. Type in this book ID **1429606177** for age-appropriate sites. You may also browse subjects by clicking on letters, or by clicking on pictures and words.
4. Click on the **Fetch It** button.

FactHound will fetch the best sites for you!

Glosario

antiguo — de hace muchísimo tiempo

la bolsa — bolsillo de piel en el que algunos animales llevan a sus crías

la camada — grupo de animales que nacen juntos de la misma madre

el cazador — animal que vive de cazar a otros animales

clonar — usar las células de un animal para crear otro animal idéntico

el extraño — raro o misterioso

el marsupial — animal que lleva a sus crías en una bolsa

merodear — moverse rápida y sigilosamente

la presa — animal que es cazado por otro animal para comérselo

prosperar — vivir fácilmente y bien

el ualabí — animal australiano que parece un cangurito

el wombat — animal australiano que parece un osito

Sitios de Internet

FactHound te brinda una manera divertida y segura de encontrar sitios de Internet relacionados con este libro. Hemos investigado todos los sitios de FactHound. Es posible que algunos sitios no estén en español.

Se hace así:
1. Visita *www.facthound.com*
2. Elige tu grado escolar.
3. Introduce este código especial ID **1429606177** para ver sitios apropiados a tu edad, o usa una palabra relacionada con este libro para hacer una búsqueda general.
4. Haz un clic en el botón **Fetch It**.

¡FactHound buscará los mejores sitios para ti!

Index

Índice